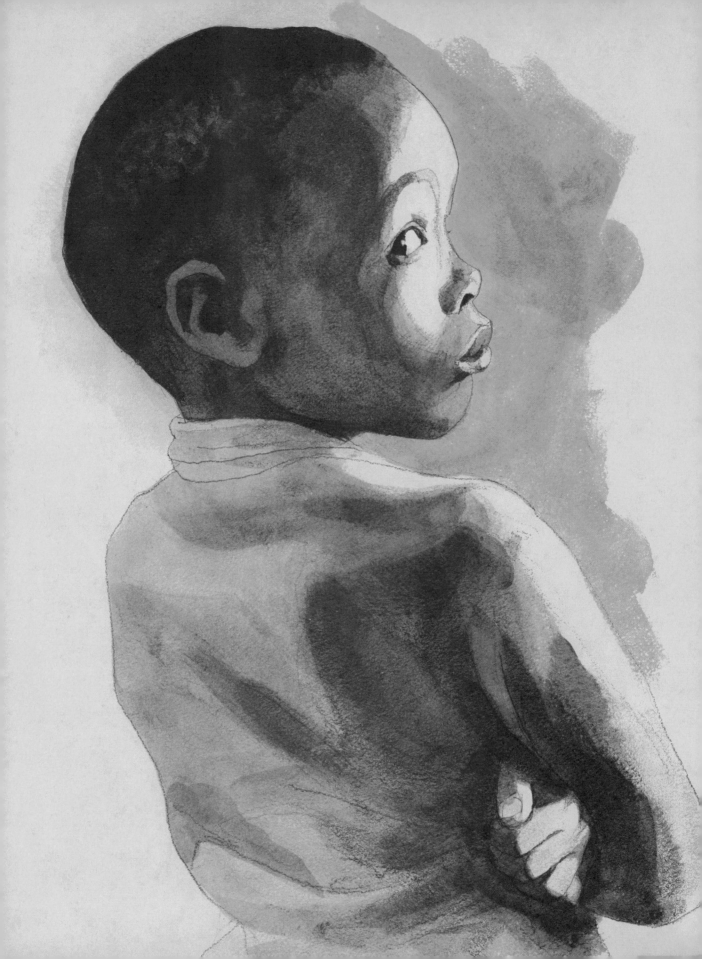

SAM

by Ann Herbert Scott

Drawings by Symeon Shimin

Philomel Books • New York

For Peter Scott and Toby Shimin

Published in 1992 by Philomel Books, a division of The Putnam & Grosset
Book Group, 200 Madison Avenue, New York, NY 10016.
Originally published in 1967 by McGraw-Hill Book Company, New York.
Published simultaneously in Canada.
Library of Congress Catalog Card Number: 67-22968.
ISBN 0-399-22104-2. 10 9 8 7 6 5 4 3 2

Sam wanted to play.

Everyone in his house was busy, and no one
wanted to play with him.

Sam walked into the kitchen, where his mother was peeling apples for pie. He picked up a knife from the table.

"SAM, don't touch that knife," cried his mother. "That knife is very sharp—too sharp for little boys. I don't ever want to see you touch that knife again."

Sam's mother went back to peeling apples. "Why don't you go outside and play, Sammy," she said.

Sam walked out on the porch. His big brother
George was sitting on the steps, reading his books
from school.

Sam picked up a book and turned the pages to
find a picture.

"SAM, put down that book," yelled George.
"That's *my* book, and you're not to touch it."

Sam looked as if he might cry.

"That's a book I got from school," said George, not quite so loud as before. "If you get it dirty or rip the pages, I'll be in trouble. Don't ever touch my books again. Understand?"

Sam just stood there.

"Why don't you go inside and play, Sammy," said George.

Sam went into the living room. There by the window his big sister Marcia was making clothes for her paper dolls.

Sam picked up one of the dolls and waved its hand up and down.

"SAM," screamed Marcia when she saw what he was doing. "You'll bend my doll's hand. You'll *ruin* her!"

Sam looked as if he might cry.
"You go play somewhere else, Sammy. But don't
ever touch my dolls again."

Sam just stood there.

"Why don't you go find Daddy," said Marcia.

Sam's father was sitting at his desk, reading the newspaper. Sam stood beside him for a minute. Then PING, Sam punched down a key on the typewriter.

"SAM, get your hands off that typewriter," shouted his father. "How many times must I tell you—that typewriter is not a toy for children. Typewriters are very easy to break and they cost lots of money to fix. Don't ever touch my typewriter again."

Sam's father turned back to his newspaper. "Why don't you go find Mother," he said.

Then Sam really did cry. He sat right down on the floor by his father's desk and he cried and cried and cried.

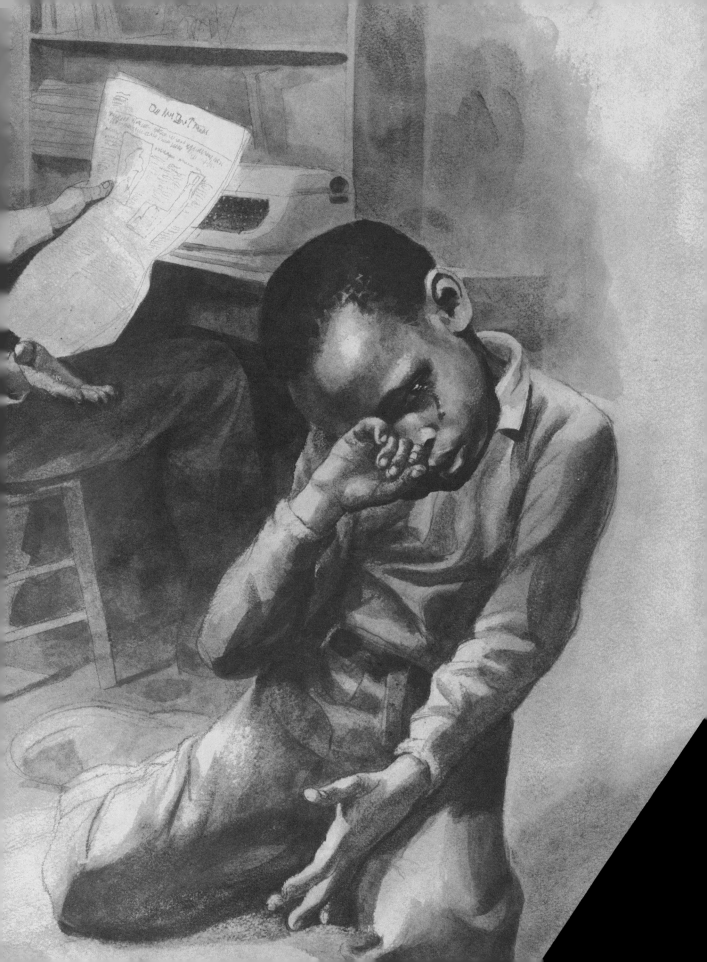

He cried so loud that his mother came
in from the kitchen and his big brother George
came in from the porch and his big sister Marcia
came in from the living room.

"What in the world is the matter with Sam?"
asked his mother.

"I think I know," said his mother, sitting down
in the rocking chair by the desk and picking up
Sam in her arms.

"I think I know, too," said George.

"I think I know, too," said Marcia.

For a minute everyone was quiet. The rocking
chair creaked back and forth as Sam curled in his
mother's arms.

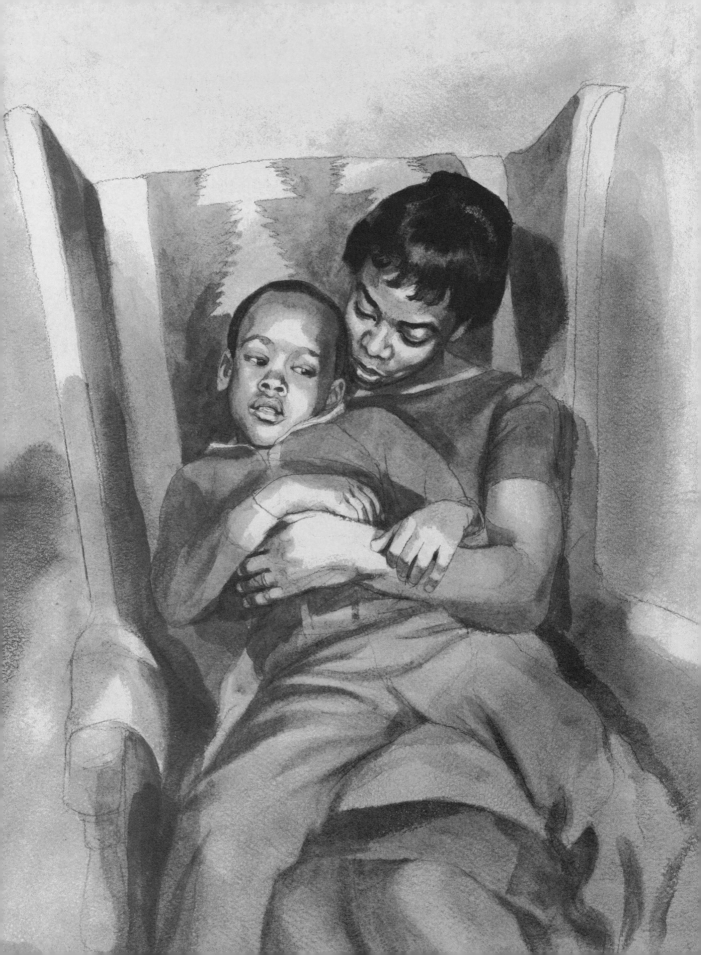

"Sammy," said his mother, "if you're not too busy, there's a job you could do for me in the kitchen."

Sam was tired of crying, so he followed his mother into the kitchen. His father and his big sister and his big brother all came along, too.

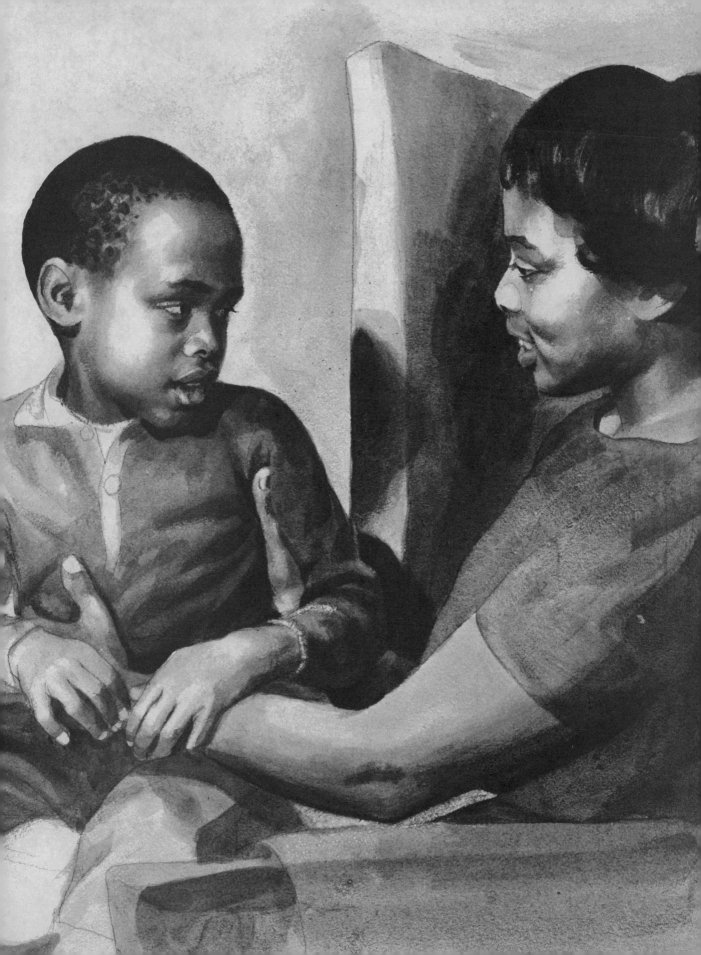

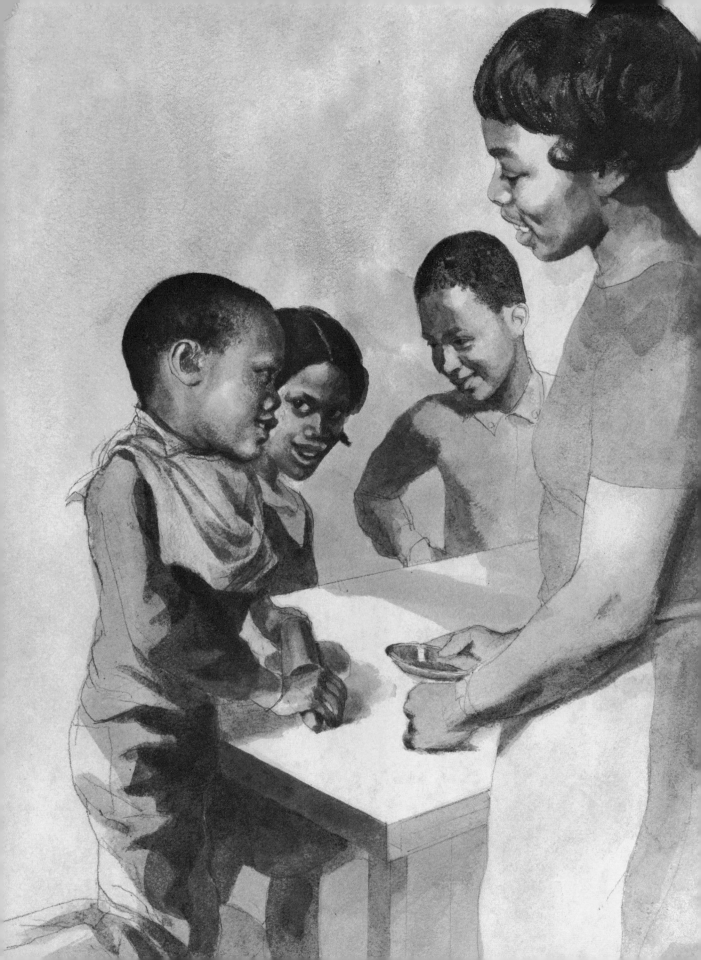

Sam's mother pulled out a tall kitchen stool so he could reach the table. Then she pinned a dish towel around his neck so he wouldn't get dirty. And then she gave him a piece of soft pie dough and a rolling pin so he could roll the dough out flat.

"There's just enough dough to fit in this little pan," said Sam's mother. "Maybe you can make a tart to bake in the oven with the pie."

"Say, that's a good job for Sam," said his father.

"He's not too little," said his sister.

"And he's not too big," said his brother.

"In fact," said his mother, "he's just the right size. And now, Sammy, what kind of jam would you like for your tart?"

"Raspberry," said Sam.